The Snowman's Wish

....

For Rob and Lijtje

First published in the United States, Great Britain, Canada, Australia, and New Zealand
in 2013 by NorthSouth Books, Inc., an imprint of NordSüd Verlag AG, CH-8005
Zürich, Switzerland.

Distributed in the United States by NorthSouth Books Inc., New York 10016.
Library of Congress Cataloging-in-Publication Data is available.
ISBN: 978-0-7358-4144-4 (trade edition)
Printed in Printed in Belgium by Proost N.V., B 2300 Turnhout, July 2013.
1 3 5 7 9 • 10 8 6 4 2
www.northsouth.com

MIX
Paper from
responsible sources
FSC
www.fsc.org
FSC® C101807

The Snowman's Wish

Harmen van Straaten

North
South

Our story begins on the deepest, darkest day of winter. . . .
Everything was covered in snow, and outside it was as cold
as ice cream.
Everybody in the little cottage was fast asleep.

Everybody?
If you listened very carefully you could hear the soft sound of voices. It sounded like an argument.
Who could it be at this hour? It was the toys!

"Well, I live on the TOP shelf!" said the robot.
"But I'm their favorite!" the baby doll replied.
"I've been here the longest!" added the purple pony.
"That's nothing; I starred in a movie!" said the bright red car.

"In a supporting role that nobody noticed," teased the windup mouse.

To put it plainly, every toy thought it was the best.

Every toy?

Down on the bottom shelf was a snowman in a globe made of glass.

"I can make it snow," he said timidly.

But nobody was listening to him. Poor Snowman! It hadn't snowed in his globe for ages, his music was out of tune, and nobody had played with him for such a long time, he was beginning to gather dust.

Even his old friend the elephant had started to
ignore him.
The snowman was very, very sad.

What was that? the snowman wondered, putting his ear
to his globe.

The room filled with sweet music.

"Do you want to dance with me?" sang a soft, clear voice.

The snowman had never heard anything so wonderful. He wished and wished that he could leave his globe and find out where the music was coming from. But he was trapped.

All at once a strange light appeared in the room—as though a moonbeam was shining on the snowman alone. Stranger still, he felt a breeze. He tried to tap the glass with his broom, but . . . there was nothing there! To his astonishment, he was free!

"What's going on?" the snowman called out.

"You wished you could leave your globe!" said a voice from across the room.

"And now you can," it added.

The voice came from the clock on the mantelpiece.

On top of the clock was a golden angel.

She smiled down at the snowman and said, "Now listen very carefully; you have exactly one hour, then you must get back to your globe, as it will close up again. If you're not back when the clock strikes one . . ."

"Then I will melt?" interrupted the snowman.

"You'd better get going!" said the angel. "You don't have all night."

There was no time to lose. The snowman followed the
sound of the music. He rounded a corner and stopped
in his tracks. A beautiful dancer in a pink dress was
slowly revolving around and around. She was the one
who was singing!

"Who will dance with me tonight?
Will you dance with me?
Who will dance with me tonight?"

The snowman had never seen anyone so elegant
and beautiful before.
He plucked up all his courage, gently took her
outstretched hand, and said, "I will!"

They danced and danced, twisting and twirling until they felt giddy.

"Dancing together is much more fun than dancing alone," she said.

The snowman nodded sadly. He only had a few more minutes.

"I'm sorry, but I have to go," he said, and turned to leave.

The snowman glanced back at the dancer, then headed back to his snow globe.

On his way, he passed the angel on the clock.

"I can't stay with her?" he asked.

The angel shook her head and said, "I had but one wish to grant you."

The other toys, who had been watching, started to laugh.

"Nobody wants to play with you!" said the windup mouse.

"Look at Snowball!" cried the robot.

"He thinks he can dance,"
added the baby doll.

"He certainly fell for
that one," said the red car
with a grin.

The snowman felt tears prick his eyes.
The toys were right. What could the
beautiful dancer possibly see in him?
He must have been dreaming.

The snowman was back at his old snow globe.
He looked around in despair.
He didn't want to go inside!
He just wanted to be with the little dancer again.

Dong! The clock struck one. It was too late.
The snowman felt a drop fall from his forehead.
Soon a puddle began to form at his feet.

All at once he heard a clear voice.

"Snowman, where are you?"

It was the dancer!

"Here I am!" said the melting snowman.

The dancer saw the puddle of water around him and was horrified.

"Snowman!" she cried.

The snowman pointed to the angel and said, "She granted me one wish—the one hour I spent with you. It was the best hour of my life."

The dancer looked up at the clock and said, "Oh, dear angel!
May I also make a wish?"

"I would like to be with you always," she said to the snowman.

The snowman closed his eyes.

He heard beautiful music.

The music was coming from his snow globe!

Slowly, he opened his eyes. . . .

The dancer stood next to him. The snowman wrapped his
scarf around her and asked softly, "Would you like to dance
with me?"

"Yes," said the little dancer. "Forever."

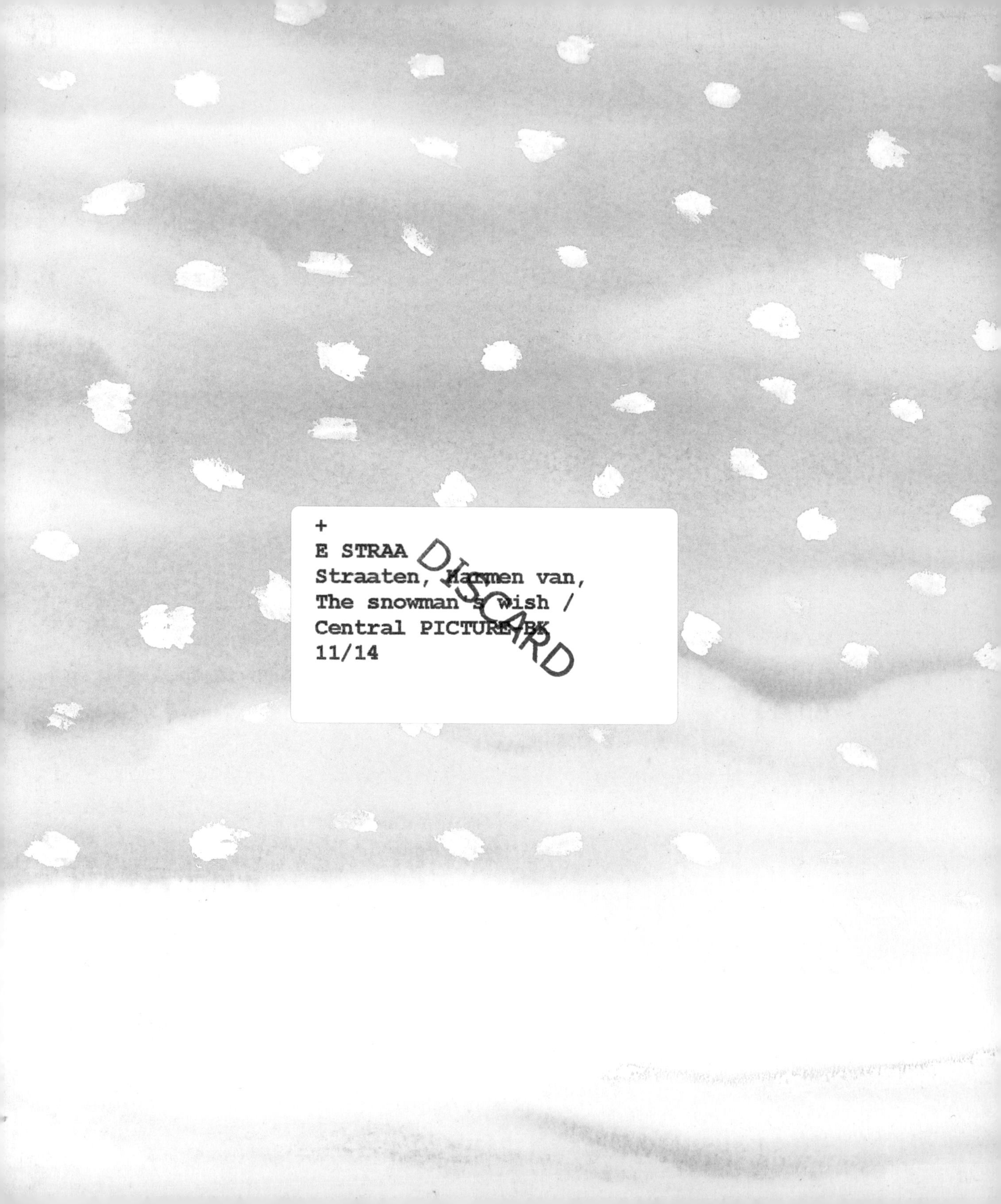